Shivers and Ca[s]: Jim's Corner Market

Janet G. Sims

Illustrations by Kalpart

Strategic Book Publishing and Rights Co.

This book was written for my husband, Jim,

who is looking down on me from Heaven.

His words for me would be,

"Thanks, Janelle, my beautiful brown-eyed girl."

Shivers was a very funny little kitten. She had long, fluffy, light grey hair with white hair on her face and chest.

4

She had brothers and sisters, but she was the only grey one in the bunch. She didn't try to be funny. But everywhere she went it seems she made everyone laugh. She was always doing unusual things that no one else would think to do. That is what made her so different from all the other little kittens. You might say she had her own "special" paersonality.

Now Shivers' best friend was a little puppy named Casey. His long hair was also light grey and he also had white on his face and chest.

6

They could almost pass for twins except Casey was a puppy and Shivers a kitten. He lived next door alone, without any of his brothers and sisters. That is why they became such good friends. He was always doing things to get himself in trouble. Casey didn't mean to get into trouble, but things sometimes turned out that way. But Shivers was always around to help him. Together they managed to get away safe, and Shivers was always there to do something funny to make him laugh.

One day Shivers decided she wanted to go to the Jim's Corner Market. She stopped to ask Casey to go with her. As he turned to follow her,

Casey knocked off a plant that was sitting on the porch. It broke, spilling the dirt and the plant onto the ground.

9

"Run Casey," laughed Shivers, "before Mr. Broom strikes!"

So off they ran toward the pond that they had to go past to get to the store. It was located on the other side of Casey's house. So, across the yard and to the top of the big hill they ran. As they started down the hill, Shivers stumbled over a toy truck that laid hidden in the grass.

Losing her balance, she started to roll all the way to the bottom of the hill. Casey ran after her laughing.

11

As he reached the bottom, he stumbled over a rock and fell into the pond. Casey realized too late that he should have been more careful being that close to a pond.

"Help me, Shivers," begged Casey.

Shivers was laughing as she jumped up and ran to the edge of the pond. She saw a lily pad close to Casey, but what she didn't know was that the lily pad would not hold her up. Shivers leapt onto it and suddenly, Shivers found herself sinking face first into the pond.

Shivers and Casey managed to get out of the pond safely and dry off. All the swimming had made them hungry so off they finally went to Jim's Corner Market. They knew that they could get something good to eat there.

When they arrived, the door was closed so they sat down to wait for it to be opened again. The wait was not long. When the door opened, Casey and Shivers ran inside. Shivers knew just where to go to find what she was hungry for, and Casey knew where to find what he wanted also.

So off they ran in different directions to get their snacks. They knew they had to move quickly before Jim, the owner of the store, would see them and throw them out.

Shivers was headed to the fresh fish section. When she got there, she sat down in front of the counter to pick out the fish she wanted.

When she had finally decided which one, she leapt up onto the counter, grabbed her fish, then jumped back onto the floor. Then she ran like lightning to the front door to make her big exit.

15

Casey found the pet food aisle, and there right in front of him was a big tub of doggie biscuits. What a surprise!

It was just what he was looking for. He stood up on his back legs and put his front paws on the edge of the big tub. He grabbed a doggie biscuit and off he ran to find the front door before someone caught him.

When Shivers and Casey reached the door, there stood Jim holding a broom.

18

They both stopped so quickly that the snacks they had grabbed flew out of their mouths. The snacks landed in each other's mouth. Casey swallowed the fish while Shivers ate the biscuit.

Casey made a funny face because he didn't like the taste of fish, but Shivers liked the biscuit. The door suddenly opened, and they both ran out as fast as they could, laughing as they ran.

Shivers and Casey ran until they reached the park. Now they were both thirsty after having their snack and running from the broom.

Right in the middle of the park was a wading pool. So, they decided to go take a closer look. They walked over to the edge, and they found what they needed to quench their thirst. They had found cool water.

Shivers and Casey moved closer to the wading pool to get a cool drink. They bent over so they could reach the water easier. Just as they lowered their heads to get a drink, a big round ball came flying through the air and landed in the water.

The big ball caused water to splash everywhere, including all over Shivers and Casey.

"What was that, Casey?" asked Shivers as they both moved away from the wading pool.

Casey began to shake all over to get rid of the water that had splashed on him by the ball, while Shivers sat down and used her front paw to remove the water from her face.

Casey didn't mind getting wet because it had cooled him off.

Shivers hated being wet because she was a cat, but it had cooled her off too.

While they were still sitting there in the park cleaning up, a big grey squirrel ran in front of them. It was headed for the big oak tree to get an acorn to eat for its lunch.

"Look Shivers, there's a squirrel!" Seeing the squirrel running past excited Casey. He began barking very loudly, which made the squirrel run even faster to get to the oak tree. Seeing the squirrel and hearing Casey barking made Shivers get excited too.

"Yay, a squirrel!" she shouted. Then she jumped up and began to chase the big grey squirrel as it ran toward the oak tree. This is always one of her favorite things to do while in the park.

When the squirrel reached the oak tree, it climbed up the tree trunk then onto the biggest branch.

Shivers ran as fast as she could, but the squirrel was faster. It was already on the big limb before Shivers even reached the tree. As she was climbing up the tree trunk, the squirrel grabbed an acorn then climbed even higher to the top of the tree. When Shivers reached the big limb, she could no longer see the squirrel that she was chasing.

As Shivers stood on the big limb, she looked down to see Casey waiting for her on the ground.

30

He had stopped barking when the squirrel disappeared. Now she realized that she needed to go back down, and climbing down a tree was always harder than climbing up one.

Standing on that limb looking down at the ground made her stop and think. She shouldn't have climbed that high in a tree, because it might turn out to be very dangerous. Now she had to be very careful going back down so she wouldn't fall and get hurt.

As she turned around to start back down, her foot slipped, and she fell, landing right on top of Casey.

Casey let out a yelp, while Shivers groaned. Shivers was lucky that Casey was there to break her fall, and that neither one got hurt. After they both stood and began to move about without feeling any pain, they both began to laugh about what had just happened. Both had been lucky this time.

Now it was getting late, so it was time for the two to head back home.

It had been a long and busy day for both Shivers and Casey so they both began to walk back home together. They had enjoyed their day, and both were very hungry. They knew they would find dinner waiting for them at home. Shivers said goodbye to Casey when they reached his doghouse. Since they lived next door to each other, Shivers did not have a long way to go. Shivers was glad to be back home, and when she reached her backyard she was a very happy cat. Now she could eat her dinner. And after she ate, she would take a long nap.

Shivers was happy to have a friend like Casey and she fell asleep thinking about the next adventure they'd have going to Jim's Corner Market.

CPSIA information can be obtained
at www.ICGtesting.com
Printed in the USA
BVHW020830200921
617100BV00002B/15

9 781682 354582